W9-BRT-223

Perseus and the Monstrous Medusa

HEROES IN TRAINING

Perseus and the Monstrous Medusa

Joan Holub and
Suzanne Williams

LA GRANGE PUBLIC LIBRARY
10 WEST COSSITT
LA GRANGE, ILLINOIS 60525

Aladdin NEW YORK LONDON
TORONTO SYDNEY NEW DELHI

J
HEROES
STEP UP

APR '16

This book is a work of fiction. Any references to historical events, real people, or real places are used fictitiously. Other names, characters, places, and events are products of the authors' imagination, and any resemblance to actual events or places or persons, living or dead, is entirely coincidental.

ALADDIN
An imprint of Simon & Schuster Children's Publishing Division
1230 Avenue of the Americas, New York, NY 10020
First Aladdin hardcover edition April 2016
Text copyright © 2016 by Joan Holub and Suzanne Williams
Illustrations copyright © 2016 by Craig Phillips
Also available in an Aladdin paperback edition.
All rights reserved, including the right of reproduction
in whole or in part in any form.
ALADDIN is a trademark of Simon & Schuster, Inc.,
and related logo is a registered trademark of Simon & Schuster, Inc.
For information about special discounts for bulk purchases,
please contact Simon & Schuster Special Sales
at 1-866-506-1949 or business@simonandschuster.com.
The Simon & Schuster Speakers Bureau can bring authors to your live event.
For more information or to book an event,
contact the Simon & Schuster Speakers Bureau at 1-866-248-3049
or visit our website at www.simonspeakers.com.
Jacket designed by Karina Granda
Interior designed by Mike Rosamilia
The text of this book was set in Adobe Garamond Pro.
Manufactured in the United States of America 0316 FFG
2 4 6 8 10 9 7 5 3 1
Library of Congress Control Number 2016932132
ISBN 978-1-4814-3516-1 (hc)
ISBN 978-1-4814-3515-4 (pbk)
ISBN 978-1-4814-3517-8 (eBook)

For our heroic readers:
Tobey I., Kristen S., Zubin N., Ela N., Lily-Ann S., Megan D.,
Brenden S., Caitlin R., Hannah R., Tiffany W., Justin W.,
Christine D.-H., Khanya S., Sven S., Coen S., Keira J.,
Keny Y., Koko Y., Tait L., Tristan and Jake B., Mia and
Alyssa T., the Andrade family, Raymond H., Kenzo S.,
Raven G., Patricia P., Nick R., Rebecca S., Katherine Q.,
Marilyn M., Kathy C., Valerie U., Angela L., Bibi L.,
Gabriella G., and you!
—J. H. and S. W.

⚡ Contents ⚡

Greetings,
Mortal Readers,

I am Pythia, the Oracle of Delphi, in Greece. I have the power to see the future. Hear my prophecy:

Ahead, I see dancers lurking. Wait—make that *danger* lurking. (The future can be blurry, especially when my eyeglasses are foggy.)

Anyhoo, beware! Titan giants seek to rule all of Earth's domains—oceans, mountains, forests, and the depths of the Underwear.

Oops—make that *Underworld*. Led by King Cronus, they are out to destroy us all!

Yet I foresee hope. A band of rightful rulers called Olympians will arise. Though their size and youth are no match for the Titans, they will be giant in heart, mind, and spirit. They await their leader—a very special boy. One who is destined to become king of the gods and ruler of the heavens.

If he is brave enough.

And if he and his friends work together as one. And if they can learn to use their new amazing flowers—um, amazing *powers*—in time to save the world!

CHAPTER ONE

In Search of Hairy Snakes

Apollo strummed his lyre and sang as he and eleven other Olympians—six boys and six girls, all of them about ten years old—marched along the coastline of Greece:

> *"The hairy snakes, the hairy snakes!*
> *We'll find them soon, make no mistake.*
> *But will they have hair, cute and curly?*
> *Or hair that's wild and whirly twirly?*

I wonder if it's short and neat?

Or if it hangs down to their feet?"

Zeus, the black-haired, blue-eyed leader of the group, sighed in annoyance. Apollo had been singing about the Olympians' current quest for the last two miles. "Will you please stop singing that song?" Zeus asked him.

"Yeah, snakes don't have long hair. Or feet," Hera scoffed. She and Zeus's two other sisters, Demeter and Hestia, were walking right behind Zeus, Apollo, and gray-eyed Athena. Zeus's brothers, Hades and Poseidon, trooped side by side a little ways back of them.

"Well, these snakes are probably Creatures of Chaos, so they might have feet," said Apollo. "You don't know."

Ares, who came next with the blond and beautiful Aphrodite, waved his spear. "I hope they're giant, hairy jungle snakes! That would be a great fight!" The god of war's red eyes shone at the thought.

Zeus shuddered. In his humble opinion, there'd been far too much fighting during all their other quests. As leader of the Olympians, he felt it was his duty to help them *avoid* fights whenever possible. Unfortunately they didn't always have that choice.

"Let's just hope they're not *poisonous* snakes," called out Artemis, who was Apollo's twin sister. With a golden bow and a quiver of silver arrows slung across her back, she was marching alongside her brother.

"I bet I could make a mechanical snake," mused Hephaestus as he struggled to keep pace with the others. He'd crafted the cool silver cane that helped him walk. It was carved with wicked-looking skulls. He was a genius when it came to crafting mechanical metal machinery, tools, and creatures.

"Can we please stop talking about snakes?" Zeus asked the group. "I know Pythia told us to find hairy ones. But she's never exactly right when she sends us on a quest. For all we know, we could be looking for . . . fairy cakes instead of hairy snakes. Or something like that, anyway."

Ares frowned. "Fairy cakes? That wouldn't be much of a fight."

"Well, I'm tired of fighting," said Hestia, the goddess of the hearth. "I wish these quests were over and we could all go home."

"We're Olympians!" cried Poseidon, whose eyes were as turquoise as the sea. "We have no home—not until we defeat King Cronus and the other Titans." Titans were giants as tall as oak trees.

"And the Cronies," Ares added. Cronies were the

army of half-giants who obeyed King Cronus. "We've got to defeat them, too!"

It was from Pythia, the Oracle at Delphi— who could see the future but not always clearly— that the Olympians had learned their destiny. Which was to save Greece from evil Cronus and the cruel Titans. Then the Olympians would rule in King Cronus's place. And it was also from Pythia that Zeus had found out he was destined to become the ruler of everyone. The number one guy in charge.

At the moment, though, Zeus would gladly have let someone else take charge. And not just because he didn't want another fight on his hands. No. He could handle another fight if he had to . . . as long as it didn't involve *snakes*. Especially hairy, scary, and possibly poisonous ones. He had faced enemies as tall as mountains, but snakes? He shuddered.

"Let me just say that when we are finally done with all our quests and have defeated our enemies, I plan to ban snakes!" Zeus declared.

Aphrodite's blue eyes went round. "I've never seen one. What do they look like?"

"What, were you born yesterday?" Hera asked. Then she grinned. "Oh, right! You were."

She wasn't just teasing. It was true. Pretty Aphrodite had risen from the ocean the day before on a mound of bubbles. There were still a lot of things she didn't know about the world.

"Snakes are like worms, only way bigger," explained Hades. He was the ruler of the Under-world, a gloomy, smelly place belowground. "They have fangs that can bite you and some-times poison you, and they slither along silently so you don't know they're coming."

"Oh, I see," said Aphrodite, sounding blissfully

unconcerned. Then she asked, "What's a worm?"

"Can we please talk about something else?" Zeus pleaded.

"Ooh, Boltbrain is afraid of snakes," Hera teased in a singsong voice.

Usually Zeus could put up with her teasing, but not about this. "Just forget it!" He stomped ahead of the group and kept on marching. The path they were on wound along the top of a ridge. Down below, he could see ocean waves lapping against the sandy shore.

Athena ran up to him. "Listen, I know you don't want to talk about snakes right now, but I need to tell you something."

Zeus sighed. "What?"

"Well, it's about the aegis," she said. She opened the front of her cloak to reveal the shiny, gold shield she wore over her chest. Decorated with gold studs, the aegis was a magical object. Hera had found it in a Titan's house, and Pythia said it belonged to both Zeus and Athena.

"You know that image that appears on the aegis sometimes? The one that turned the spiders into stone?" Athena asked.

Zeus nodded. Sometimes the face of a terrifying woman with snakes on her head appeared on the shield. That image had recently scared off some spiders that had wanted to munch the Olympians for dinner.

Zeus stopped walking as something dawned on him. "Hey! The woman on that shield! You think she could be real? You think her snakes are the ones Pythia meant us to find?" he asked Athena. The rest of the Olympians had caught up to Athena and him and were all listening now.

Hephaestus leaned on his silver cane. "A real

woman with live snake hair?" he snorted. "Who ever heard of that? It's crazy!"

"Well, I had never heard of metal beasts that were alive, either, until I met you," Zeus told him. They'd found Hephaestus on an island, where he'd terrorized them with mechanical beasts such as a silver lion and a gold dog.

"Those creatures were the result of my genius," Hephaestus boasted. "But snake hair? That's just not natural."

"Neither are men who hop around on one foot, or women with wings and beaks," Hera pointed out. "But we've seen those before, too."

"I don't think we'll really know what we're looking for until we find it," Demeter said thoughtfully. "That's how it always seems to work out."

Poseidon yawned, then called to Zeus. "Yo, Bro! It's gonna be dark soon. Can we find a place to camp?"

Zeus scanned the land up ahead. The path they were on forked in two directions. The right path hugged the coast, and the left one led to what looked like a large orchard. Before he could decide which way they should go, Hera stepped up beside him. "I'll handle it!" she told him.

She took a peacock feather—her magical object—from her pocket. "Feather, show us what's ahead, so we can safely go to bed," she chanted. The feather only obeyed her when she spoke in rhyme. At her command it flew off down the coastal path.

"You know, technically, we don't sleep in beds when we camp," Apollo pointed out.

"I know that," Hera snapped. "But 'bed' rhymes with 'ahead.' And anyway, everyone knows that 'going to bed' means 'going to sleep.'"

"Hey, you're the one who got all up in my face about snakes with feet," Apollo reminded her. "If you're going be picky about my rhymes, then I can be picky about *yours*."

Hera frowned in annoyance. *Boys*, she mouthed to Demeter and Hestia, and both girls giggled.

Zeus just rolled his eyes. The Olympians were always bickering among themselves. But fortunately, when push came to shove, they always came together as a team.

"My feather's back!" Hera announced as it whooshed into her hand a few minutes later. When she gazed into the peacock feather's colorful eye, a look of alarm spread across her face.

"Cronies are coming!" she yelled.

CHAPTER TWO

Magic All Around

There! I see them!" cried Hades. Sure enough, two half-giant Cronies as big as apple trees came charging down the coastline toward them. Both of the muscled brutes held long spears. Sunlight gleamed off their metal helmets. They were scary dudes!

"Prepare to die, Olympians!" the one with the spear yelled.

"Yeah!" his buddy echoed, waving his club.

Zeus's hand instantly grabbed the dagger-sized lightning bolt that hung from his belt. When no one else had been able to, he had pulled the zigzag-shaped blade from a stone in Pythia's temple in Delphi. Now it was his magical object, and it had never let him down.

"Bolt, large!" Zeus commanded.

The thunderbolt immediately grew until it was longer than Zeus was tall. When he pointed it at the two Cronies, it sparked with electric energy. "Blast 'em!" he yelled.

Zap! A jagged charge of electricity hit the first Crony. "Ow!" yelped the half giant. Cartwheeling his arms, he fell backward. *Thump!* He slammed into the second Crony.

"Watch it, blockhead!" yelled the second one, but it was too late. The force of the zap sent both Cronies toppling over. They rolled down the hilly coastline, tumbling head over behind,

screaming at each other the whole way down.

Splash! They landed in the ocean.

"That ought to cool you off!" shouted Zeus.

' The other Olympians hollered and cheered. They'd all drawn their various weapons and magical objects too, but it turned out that only Zeus's lightning bolt had been needed this time.

"You'll be sorry!" one of the Cronies promised.

Ares laughed and shook his spear. "We're not scared!"

Poseidon raised his trident, a three-pronged spear that was his magical object. "Yeah, bring it on, you drips!"

"The coast is clear now. And so is the orchard," Hera said, gazing into her feather's eye.

"Let's try the orchard," said Hestia. "There'll be fruit to eat."

"Okay, let's get moving," Zeus said. "Before any more Cronies show up!

As they headed off, Athena grabbed a fallen tree branch with lots of leaves on it. She began sweeping the footprints they were leaving. "I'll brush our tracks away as we walk, so our enemies can't track us."

"Good idea," Zeus said.

Athena grinned. "They don't call me the goddess of cleverness for nothing."

Zeus's thunderbolt shrank to dagger size again, and he returned it to his belt. "Nice job, Bolt," he said, giving it a pat. As they marched on, he grabbed his second magical object—the oval stone amulet that he wore on a cord around his neck. "Chip, find us a safe place to camp in the orchard up ahead."

Sparkling bubbles trailed behind Aphrodite as she skipped over to him just then.

"Ooh, let me see your pretty magic rock!" she begged sweetly.

Zeus held up the amulet so she could see it better. "Afety-sip is-thip ay-wip!" Chip said in its special language. A glowing green arrow appeared on the stone's smooth surface.

Aphrodite jumped back in surprise. "I've never seen a talking rock before!" she exclaimed.

Hera rolled her eyes. "It just gave us directions in Chip Latin. You move the first letter of each word to the end of the word and add 'ip.'"

"Oh, I get it. So did Chip just say, 'Skip the pasty ape'?" Aphrodite guessed.

Zeus laughed. "No. It was 'Safety this way.'"

Now Ares ran up. He pushed his way between Aphrodite and Zeus. "Want to see what my magic object can do, Aphrodite? I call it the Spear of Fear. Because our enemies should fear it!"

Competing for Aphrodite's attention as well, Hephaestus thrust his cane between her and

Ares. "My cane isn't magic, but aren't the skulls on it awesome? I crafted it myself," he boasted.

Aphrodite smiled at all three boys.

Phwwwt! Something sliced through the air, right past their heads! It was a silver arrow. It whizzed onward and into the branches of an apple tree at the edge of the orchard. There, it shook several apples loose to the ground.

"Can your rock, spear, or cane do that?" Artemis asked the boys who'd been fawning over Aphrodite. She grinned as her arrow flew back to her.

Before Ares and Hephaestus could reply, Poseidon laughed. "How did you know I was getting hungry?" he asked her, running off to grab some apples.

"We're all hungry," said Hera. She and some of the others grabbed apples to snack on too.

Zeus looked down at Chip. "Almost there."

Twenty minutes later, a green *X* finally appeared on Chip. That meant they had reached a good camping spot.

"Okay, this is it," Zeus announced.

They had stopped in an open area right in the middle of the huge orchard. A stream bubbled through the clearing, which was surrounded by apple, orange, and fig trees.

"Good job, Chip!" said Demeter, looking around at the trees. "There's plenty to eat here."

"Why does it matter?" Hephaestus asked her. "With those magic seeds you carry in your pouch, you could grow us stuff to eat anytime, right?"

"I don't have many seeds," Demeter explained. "So I use them only when necessary."

Poseidon ran toward the stream. "I see fish jumping in there!" he shouted. "I'm going to catch us some dinner!" His magical trident could cause tidal waves and make water bubble up where there had been none before. It was also great at spearing fish.

"Hey, I can spear fish too!" cried Ares, joining him.

Hestia began to collect branches. "I'll get a fire going," she said. Her magical object, a torch, burned with an eternal flame.

"And I'll loosen some more fruit from these trees," Artemis offered, stringing her bow again.

Hades looked down at the magic helmet he carried—the Helm of Darkness. Whenever he put it on, he became invisible. "I'd use my magic helmet to help with dinner," he said, "but I don't see how turning invisible would be useful."

"Maybe you could sneak up on the fish and grab them?" Hera joked.

Hades grinned. "That's not such a bad idea. I bet it would work! Hey, Fishboy and Spearhead,

wait for me!" He ran off to join Poseidon and Ares.

Zeus smiled to see everyone using their magical objects and working together as a team again. It had made him so happy when he had first discovered that he had brothers and sisters. Sure, it was weird that their father was King Cronus and their mom was the not-mean queen Rhea. But Zeus had grown up all alone, raised by some bees and a goat. So having a family now felt great—even if it was kind of complicated.

When Poseidon, Ares, and Hades came back to the camp with fish, Zeus took his thunderbolt from his belt again. Leaving Bolt small, he aimed it at one of the three big fish stuck on the points of Poseidon's trident.

"Fry some fish, Bolt!" Zeus commanded.

Zap! Soon the three tasty-smelling fish were sizzling. Next Bolt flew to fry the fish Ares had speared and those Hades had caught in his hands when he'd gone invisible. *Zap! Zap!* Mission accomplished, Bolt zoomed back to Zeus.

Zeus smiled down at his magical object as he slipped it back into his belt. "What would I do without you, Bolt?"

Meanwhile Hephaestus and Apollo sat on the ground and watched Hestia start a campfire. "So, I guess we're the only two guys here without magical objects, right?" Hephaestus asked Apollo. "I mean, my cane is pretty cool, but it can't actually do magic."

Apollo nodded. "Same with my lyre. But at least it helps me make beautiful music." He strummed his lyre and began to sing.

"The heroes in training got ready to eat.
They had hungry bellies and very tired feet.

And while I sit here and watch the fish

bake,

I'll sing about anything but hairy

snakes. . . ."

Aphrodite joined the two boys, sitting down beside them. "My golden apple is supposed to be magic, but I'm not sure what it does." She held up the shiny gold apple she always carried in her pocket. "I'd give it to one of you since you want magical objects so badly. But the one thing I've figured out about it so far is that it won't let me give it away."

"Why don't you try doing something else with it while we're waiting for dinner?" suggested Apollo. "Like, maybe it can do spells?"

Aphrodite wrinkled her brow. "Okay," she said after a minute. She lifted the apple above her head. "Apple, can you make it rain cookies?"

She looked hopefully at the sky, but no cookie rain came. No actual rain either, for that matter. She sighed. Lowering her arm, she tossed the apple from her left hand to her right one. Everyone gasped when, suddenly, gold coins began to rain down from the sky and onto the grass!

"Oh, look! Cookies!" Aphrodite said, picking one up. She bit it and then frowned. "Oh, I guess they're not cookies after all."

"No! They're coins. They're way better than cookies!" Hephaestus exclaimed.

"Nothing's better than cookies," Aphrodite insisted.

"What? Don't you get it? We'll never have to go hungry or beg villagers for food again. We can buy whatever we want!" Apollo told her.

"Including cookies?" asked Aphrodite, perking up.

"Yeah! Flipping flounder, we're rich!" Poseidon

cheered. Everyone began excitedly helping to collect the raining gold coins into a small pile.

"Aphrodite, try tossing the apple to your other hand now," Zeus suggested.

Aphrodite obeyed, tossing the apple to her left hand. The coins stopped raining. She tossed the apple back to her right hand. The coins rained again. She tossed the apple to her left hand. No coins.

She let out a bubbly laugh. "So all I have to do is toss it from one hand to the other to start and stop the coins from raining down from the sky!" she said. After all the Olympians congratulated Aphrodite, they turned back to making dinner.

Demeter approached Athena. "Can you make some more pickled olives for us?"

"Mmm, yeah," said Hades, overhearing. "They're tasty."

"Please?" Demeter asked, and there was such

a look of pleading in her green eyes that Athena couldn't resist.

"Sure," Athena agreed.

When she turned, her cloak opened a little and Zeus saw the aegis. The scary snakehead face didn't appear on it. *Good!* That thing made him almost as jittery as real snakes!

First, Athena stuck a stick into the dirt at her feet. Next, she got out her Thread of Cleverness. It was yet another magical object, and it could form words and send messages.

"Pickled olives," she told it. Instantly her thread twisted itself into cursive letters that formed those words. *Whoosh!* The stick grew into a bushy tree with small, green olives. They dropped to the ground, where they shriveled into delicious, pickled olives.

Demeter clapped her hands. "Cool! Thank you!" She, Hestia, and Hades scooped up the olives and took them over to the fire. The other Olympians had gathered around it by now, since the sun had gone down and it was getting cold. Poseidon began to pass around chunks of the flash-fried fish.

Zeus took a piece to Athena when he noticed that she hadn't come over.

"Thanks," she told him. She ate it right away, then sighed and looked down at the aegis she still wore.

"Worrying about that monster snake face?" he asked her.

She nodded. "It's weird that it hasn't appeared again. I'm starting to wonder if it only pops up when we're in danger. Maybe it's a . . . premonition, a *warning* of coming danger."

"If that's true, I'm glad it's not appearing right now!" Zeus said. He sounded so relieved about this that Athena laughed. "Not that I'm scared

of danger or anything," he added quickly. In truth, though, he was still hoping Pythia had been mistaken and they were actually supposed to find fairy cakes instead of hairy snakes.

Just then, a small brown snake slithered right between Athena and him, heading for the apple trees.

"Eeeek!" Zeus cried, jumping back.

Of course Hera witnessed the whole thing and began laughing. "Way to go, Boltbreath! If a little snake like that scares the pants off you, how are you going to deal with big, scary, hairy snakes?"

Zeus was wondering the same thing himself!

CHAPTER THREE

What's the Deal with Perseus?

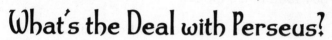

Early the next morning the Olympians cleaned up their camp and headed out. Guided by Chip's arrow, they passed through the orchard again and then swung back toward the coastline. Soon they spotted a small fishing village up ahead.

"Any Cronies around?" Zeus asked Hera.

She sent her feather out to check. "All clear," she reported once it was back.

"Then let's go!" Zeus called out. The twelve Olympians marched into the village, which was bustling with activity.

"Aphrodite, can you give me some of those coins your golden apple rained down yesterday?" Ares asked. "We're going to need some money to buy food and supplies."

"Sure!" she answered with her usual sweet smile. She reached into her pocket. Sparkling bubbles floated around her as she tossed some coins to Ares. He caught them in both hands.

"Thanks!"

"Look, cheese!" Demeter cried when they got to a stall stocked with various cheeses.

Ares handed her a gold coin. "Don't get anything too stinky."

"Hey, I like stinky!" Hades protested.

"I think this coin will be enough to get all kinds of cheeses, stinky and nonstinky,"

Demeter assured him. She approached the stall and smiled at the elderly man who was minding it. "Cheese, please," she said, holding out the coin.

The man's eyes grew wide. He took the coin and bit it. Satisfied that it was real gold, he said, "Sure, this coin will buy more than what is in my entire stall. But I'm afraid I don't have many coins for change."

Aphrodite skipped over. "It doesn't matter. You can keep the coin! Just give us two hunks of your lovely cheese."

"Stinky, please!" said Hades.

"And also not-so-stinky!" added Ares.

Zeus had a thought. "And maybe our coin will also buy us some information?" he said to the cheese man.

The man nodded eagerly, looking thrilled about getting to keep the entire coin.

"Have you ever seen or heard of any . . . hairy snakes around here?" Zeus went on.

To his surprise the cheese man nodded and pointed to some snowcapped mountains in the distance. "Sure, everybody knows about the hairy snakes. I heard they live up north on one of those mountaintops. All that long, silky hair of theirs keeps 'em warm."

"Uh, thanks for the information," Zeus said, going pale at the thought.

The man wrapped two cheese wheels as big as pies in cloths. Then he gave them to Demeter.

After sniffing them both, she put one into the pack she carried. She handed the other one to Hades, who held a sack containing his helmet. "You can carry the stinky one," she said.

"Hooray!" Hades cheered.

Once they left the cheese stall they moved on to a bread stall, a vegetable stall, and a fish stall.

Zeus asked each of the vendors the same question he'd asked the cheese man. The bread guy and the vegetable lady didn't know any more information about the hairy snakes. However, the woman selling fish had more to tell.

"They live down south, by the hot springs," she explained. "They've got wild hair. It's the steam that makes it so curly whirly, you know?"

"Really?" Hera asked skeptically.

The fish seller nodded. "Seen them myself."

After moving a short distance away from the stalls, the Olympians huddled together to discuss the opposing stories they'd been told. Just then, a dark-haired mortal boy about the same age as the Olympians came to stand nearby. Zeus had noticed him earlier, following the group from stall to stall. He looked like he was trying to hear what they were saying. When Zeus frowned at him, the boy took off.

"So, the cheese man says there are hairy snakes in the mountains, and the fish woman says we have to go to the hot springs," Zeus summarized to his eleven companions. "Do you think they're just making stuff up to get gold coins?"

As they discussed the matter among themselves, Aphrodite wandered away to a stall filled with colorful silk and wool scarves. "Oooh, pretty!" she said, trying several on. She took out a gold coin.

Zeus watched as the dark-haired mortal boy approached her, his eyes on the gold. "Pretty coin," he said, smiling.

Zeus eyed the boy more closely and noticed he was wearing a pair of sandals with wings on them. He nudged Hades and Poseidon. "See that boy? I think he might be up to something."

Overhearing, Ares blustered, "Aphrodite's still

so new to the world and is easily tricked. She probably shouldn't be talking to strangers— especially ones who know she has gold on her."

Zeus, Ares, and Hades hurried over to step between the boy and Aphrodite. "Can *we* help you?" they asked the nosy mortal.

"No, but maybe *I* can help *you*," the boy replied. "I overheard you and your friends talking about hairy snakes." Zeus and the other two Olympians looked at him.

"You heard us?" Zeus's guard went up.

"Eavesdropping, huh?" Ares demanded, taking a fighting stance. "What are you, a spy for King Cronus and the Titans or something?"

"Nuh-uh. I'm Perseus," the boy said, holding out his hand to shake theirs. By now, all twelve Olympians had gathered around him. All except Aphrodite appeared suspicious, and none shook his hand. He shrugged and dropped it. "Those snakes you're looking for are dangerous. You might need some help from the Gray Triplets before you go off trying to find them."

"The Gray Triplets?" Zeus repeated. "Who are they?"

"Three sisters who live on an island far from here," Perseus replied. "They are said to know all things, so they could tell you anything you want about those hairy snakes you seek. I'll lead you to their island if you want."

Hera stepped up. "That's a nice offer, but can't you just tell us where they live instead?" Like the others in his group, Zeus sensed she didn't trust this guy.

"Well, I have a question for them too, actually," Perseus replied. "But the thing is, I don't have a boat. You have gold, though, so you can buy one. And if you'll let me hitch a ride with you, I'll lead you there. "

"Why don't you just fly?" Zeus asked, gesturing pointedly at the boy's sandals.

Perseus frowned down at his sandals. "Oh, these things? They don't work." Then he muttered, "I never should have taken them in the first place."

"Taken them?" Hera snapped. "So you *stole* them?"

"No way!" Perseus protested. "I meant I never should have taken them in *trade*. The guy I got them from, well, let's just say he wasn't completely honest."

Hera turned to Zeus. "What do you say, fearless leader? Should we buy a boat and go sailing off with this complete stranger? Or should we go wandering off to find curly haired mountain snakes or snakes with long shiny locks?"

CHAPTER FOUR

Three Teams

E xcuse us a minute," Zeus told Perseus. The Olympians moved far enough away from the boy that he wouldn't be able to hear them. Zeus held Chip in his hand.

"Chip, can you tell us if the hairy snakes Pythia told us about are up north in the mountains or south in the hot springs? Or do we need to sail away to the island where the Gray Triplets live and ask for their help?"

A glowing green arrow appeared on Chip, and for a moment Zeus had hope of an answer. But then the arrow disappeared.

"Let me try my feather," Hera suggested. She held it in her hand and spoke a rhyme. "Feather, before we travel forth, can you point us—south or north?" She gazed into the peacock feathers' eye, hoping to see a helpful vision—but there was nothing.

Hephaestus thumped his cane against the ground impatiently. "Your magic trinkets aren't going to help us," he said. "I say we split up into three groups. One can go south, one north, and one to that island with Perseus."

Zeus frowned. Hephaestus had once tried to overthrow him as leader of the Olympians. He'd given up on that but still often argued with Zeus's commands. "I don't like it when we split up," Zeus insisted. "Something bad always happens. We're stronger when we stick together."

"Even so, Hephaestus may have a point, Bro," Poseidon put in. "I mean, not so long ago there were only four of us—you, me, Hera, and Hades. Yet we still managed to outwit the Titans and Creatures of Chaos and complete our first quest."

Zeus nodded thoughtfully. "And checking out all three possibilities at once *would* save us some time."

"We could meet back at this village again after each group checks out a place," Athena suggested.

"Good plan," agreed Demeter.

"All right," Zeus said slowly. "Let's do it. My group will go with Perseus to the island." *Because I don't trust him,* he added to himself.

"I'll go with you," Athena said, giving Zeus

a look that told him she didn't exactly trust Perseus either.

"I do not like the cold, you see, so hot springs are the place for me," rhymed Apollo.

"Then I'll go to the hot springs too," Artemis said quickly. "I'm not going to be separated from my brother again."

When the twins were just three years old, they had been kidnapped by a Titan. They had eventually escaped, but had grown up apart. Only recently had they met again when the Olympians found Artemis asleep under a magic spell.

Hera spoke up. "I'll lead a third team north to the mountains."

"I'll back you up, Sis," Poseidon offered.

Demeter and Hestia whispered to each other. Then Demeter spoke. "We'll go with Hera and Poseidon," she said.

Zeus nodded. It figured that his sisters would all want to stick together. The three of them were pretty tight. "All right. We've got our mountain team set of four, and not counting Perseus, two people each on the hot springs and Gray Triplets teams," he summarized. "Since there are twelve of us, not counting Perseus, let's make it four on each team."

"The hot springs sound bubbly!" said Aphrodite. "I'd like to go there."

"I'll go too!" Ares said quickly, obviously wanting to hang out with Aphrodite some more.

Hephaestus glared at him. "But I want to go to the hot springs," he said.

"I called it first!" said Ares.

"Ares *did* call it first," Zeus said. "So, Hephaestus, you're coming with me and Athena to visit the Gray Triplets. Hades, guess you're with us too."

The decision made, Zeus waved Perseus over.

"You know I like hot places," Hades said to Zeus as Perseus joined their group. "I would have preferred the hot springs. Still, going to visit a few ladies on an island sounds pretty easy."

"Ha!" Perseus laughed a little too loudly. *What is that about*, wondered Zeus. *Does he know something he isn't telling?*

Hephaestus sidled over to Zeus. "Why can't I go to the hot springs?" he pressed.

"Four Olympians on each team," Zeus said firmly. *Although, believe me, I'd be happier if you weren't on my team*, he thought. Hephaestus could be whiny and bossy. He wasn't the easiest Olympian to get along with.

Perseus went over to Aphrodite. "We'll need a lot more coins to buy a boat. Got any more?"

Aphrodite gave him her dazzling smile. "I can make all the gold we need!" she said happily. She pulled her golden apple from her pocket and proceeded to do just that. Perseus watched, amazed.

With the additional gold Aphrodite made, the Olympians were able to get supplies for all three separate journeys. They bought food for all, plus warm clothing for the mountain team, lightweight clothes for the hot springs team, and a small boat for Zeus and his crew.

The other Olympians gathered at the dock as Perseus, Hades, Athena, and Zeus loaded their boat. (Hephaestus stubbornly refused to help. Instead, he just watched the others do it with a scowl on his face, impatiently poking the tip of his cane into the sand.)

"Well, I guess this is good-bye for a while," Hera said to Zeus. "Good luck, Boltbrain. If you do find the hairy snakes, don't mess things up."

"I'll make sure he doesn't," Hephaestus declared pompously.

"Yeah, right," Ares muttered.

Hephaestus whipped around, whacking his cane against the side of the boat. He glared at Ares. "What did you say?"

"Nothing," Ares answered innocently.

Demeter and Hestia each hugged Zeus. "Be careful, Brother," Demeter said.

"May the fire from Bolt keep you warm," Hestia added with a grin.

Poseidon punched his shoulder. "See you soon, Bro."

Zeus felt tears begin to well in his eyes, but he held them back. *I have to be strong!* he reminded himself. And anyway, it was silly to be sad. He'd miss the Olympians on the other two teams, but they'd all see one another again soon. When his team and Perseus were onboard, they pushed off, and the boat pulled away from shore.

As the eight Olympians left behind on the

sand grew smaller and smaller in the distance, Zeus felt a lump in his throat. He *had* to see them again. He *would* see them again, no matter what. But for now, he and his crew had a job to do.

He turned to Perseus. "Okay. How do we get to the island?"

CHAPTER FIVE

One Eye, One Tooth

The afternoon sun blazed overhead as Zeus, Athena, Hades, and Hephaestus sailed the boat, following Perseus's directions.

"Keep heading north," Perseus instructed. "Until we see a cluster of small islands up ahead."

A white seagull flying above them swooped down to follow the boat a short distance.

"It's such a beautiful day," Athena said, watching the bird against the backdrop of the

bright blue sky. Then she shivered. "But why do I have the feeling we're sailing toward gloom and doom?"

"Gloom and doom," Hades repeated dreamily. "Sounds like home." No place was as gloomy and more filled with doom than the Underworld!

Zeus looked at Perseus. "What exactly do you know about these Gray Triplets?" he asked.

"Oh, just that they're supposed to be very wise," Perseus said. "Nothing to be afraid of." But he looked away, avoiding Zeus's gaze, like he wasn't quite sure of the truth of his words. Or like there was something more he didn't want to say.

Soon they reached the island cluster. "It's the island farthest to the east," Perseus said. "We're almost there."

They took down the sail when they reached

shallow water around the island. Then they all rowed the rest of the way to shore.

"So where to now?" Zeus asked as they all climbed out of the boat.

"The triplets live in a cave," Perseus replied.

"Just as I feared. We're headed for gloom," Athena said.

"Probably doom, too," muttered Hephaestus.

Athena looked at Perseus. "If the three women we seek are so wise, why are they out here in the middle of nowhere, living in a cave?"

"Yeah," Hephaestus said scornfully. "They should have built a house!"

"Hey!" Zeus protested. "I grew up in a cave. They're not so bad."

Perseus looked thoughtful. "Okay. It's time I told you all I know about the Gray Triplets. There are three of them, but they only have one eye and one tooth among them."

"Awesome! Now we're talking," said Hades, his dark eyes gleaming with interest. "But wait, how do *they* talk? Do they have mouths?"

"Not sure," said Perseus.

"One eye for three faces?" Zeus asked in confusion. "You could have mentioned all this before." He wondered what else Perseus wasn't telling the group!

"They take turns with the eye," Perseus replied. "With the tooth, too." He shrugged apologetically. "Sorry I didn't tell you before. I was worried it might scare you off. These ladies can help us, I promise."

"Yeah, right," muttered Hephaestus.

Athena's gray eyes were boring into Perseus. "We don't scare easily. So, just be honest with us from now on, okay?"

"Of course! Come on. Their cave should be this way," said Perseus. He flashed a charming smile that Zeus didn't exactly trust, then headed off. Everyone followed.

The five of them pushed through leafy bushes and trees with low-hanging branches and vines as they followed a pathway that looked like it hadn't been traveled in years. After a short time they came to a cave entrance set into a tall cliff.

"This is it," Perseus murmured.

"Looks gloomy and doomy all right," Athena said with a shudder.

"What did you expect— A 'Welcome to our Cave' sign posted at the entrance?" joked Hades.

Athena just laughed. "Well, at least a 'Cave Sweet Cave' sign."

Zeus gripped Bolt as he and the others followed Perseus inside. Even though he'd grown up in a cave himself, he didn't like the idea of going into this one. What if Perseus was leading them all into some kind of trap? What if he *was* working for King Cronus?

But it was too late to worry about that now. If it was a trap, Zeus and his team would just have to fight their way out.

It was nearly pitch black inside the cave, except the faint glow of a fire up ahead. They walked toward it. Soon they saw three women hunched over a black pot as big as a bathtub, set atop a blazing fire. Each of them wore a tattered gray robe and had wild, gray hair.

As Zeus's eyes adjusted to the gloom, a creaky voice rang out. "Sisters! I smell visitors— Olympians!"

All three women turned to look. Each had a nose, ears, and a mouth, Zeus was relieved to see.

Although all the sisters might be able to *smell* the Olympians, the triplet in the center was the only one who could *see* them. She had a single

big, blue eye stuck in her forehead directly above her nose. The faces of the other two were eyeless.

"Welcome, Olympians! I'm Pemphredo," said the woman on the left who had spoken. One white tooth gleamed in her mouth.

Without warning, the triplet on the right without the eye or the tooth snatched the tooth from Pemphredo's mouth. As soon as she popped it into her own mouth she shrieked, "And I'm Deino. Enyo, give me the eye! I want to see our visitors too!"

The one in the middle named Enyo blinked at the Olympians didn't move.

"Oh, all right," said Deino after a moment. "Trade you." She pulled the tooth from her mouth and handed it to Enyo, who put it into her own mouth. Then Enyo plucked the eye from her face and handed it to Deino. Those two sisters continued trading the eye and the tooth around.

Finally Pemphredo reached out and grabbed both tooth and eye for herself. She wasted no time in inserting both into her own face, then she gazed at Perseus and the Olympians in surprise.

"Hey, you're just a bunch of kids! What are you doing all the way out here?" she asked. And then her single eye narrowed. She sniffed the air. "Wait! I smell weapons. Drop them!"

"No way!" Zeus protested. "We would never use them hurt you."

"And anyway, my cane is *not* a weapon. It helps me walk," Hephaestus argued.

"Maybe so, but you could also clobber some-one with it," Pemphredo replied. "Think about it. We're three defenseless old ladies, and there's the whole one eye thing. We can't be too careful."

Zeus hesitated, but just for a moment. They

really did look harmless, even if they were a little weird.

"Okay. Here's mine," he said, laying Bolt on the floor. Then he looked over at Hephaestus.

"Fine," Hephaestus said, laying the cane beside Bolt.

Pemphredo pointed to the sack Hades was carrying. "And that fancy hat of yours, too, young man!"

Hades clutched his sack to his chest. "My Helm of Darkness? How did you even know it was in here?"

"Our eye can see more than the average eye," the old woman answered. "Mwah, ha-ha!" she cackled.

Deino nabbed the tooth from her. "Always with the evil laugh, Pemphredo. You'll frighten them!"

Pemphredo took the tooth back. Zeus was

amazed at how swiftly they passed the tooth and eye back and forth among them.

"These Olympians don't scare easily," Pemphredo said, her blue eye fixed on Athena. "Right, girl?"

With a look of surprise, Athena nodded.

It was exactly what Athena had said to Perseus when they'd landed on shore! recalled Zeus. He and Athena exchanged a quick glance. He suspected they were both wondering the same thing. Were the old women's ears so good that they'd heard their visitors speaking from the shore just after they landed?

"Now, missy, give up that shiny shirt you're wearing, please," Pemphredo insisted.

Reluctantly Athena handed over her aegis. "All right. But it's only a shield. For defense. It's not a weapon."

"Oh, really?" Pemphredo asked, and her eye seemed to blaze right through Athena.

Did she somehow know there were times when the aegis could turn things to stone? Zeus wondered. "Okay, we've done as you asked," he told the women. "We came here because Perseus says you're all very wise. And that you might know something that could help us."

"Help you with what?" Pemphredo asked him.

"We're on a quest. Do you know where we can find hairy snakes?" Zeus asked.

Deino took the tooth for herself and said, "Yes! We do know where to find them."

Enyo grabbed the tooth, adding, "But no, we won't tell you!"

Then Pemphredo took the tooth back again. "No way, no how!"

Hephaestus took a step forward. "Now listen up!" he said, his voice rising with anger. "We've put down our weapons and we've asked you nicely. So help us, or else!"

Deino grabbed the tooth from Pemphredo. "Who said that?" she shrieked. "Give me the eye! I want to see his beastly little face for myself!"

Pemphredo plucked out the eye and handed it across to Deino. But when Deino opened her hand, nothing was there.

"I said give me the eye!" Deino demanded.

Pemphredo took the tooth, then replied, "But I did!"

Deino took the tooth back. "But I don't have it!" she wailed. "Our eye! Our eye! Where is our eye?"

Zeus started to ask if it could have fallen into the cauldron since the women had been passing both the eye and the tooth back and forth over it. But then Perseus stepped forward.

"You mean this eye?" Perseus asked, opening his hand to show her the big, blue eye he held. Zeus had almost forgotten the mortal boy

was with them since he'd stayed quietly in the background the whole time they'd been inside the cave.

"How'd you do that?" Hades asked the sneaky boy.

Perseus ignored him. "I have your eye, ladies. And I will give it back to you, unharmed. But first you must tell us where to find the hairy snakes."

Enyo had the tooth now. "Fine," she said. "We will tell you. But if you do not give us our eye back, a terrible fate will befall you."

"I promise to give it back," said Perseus. "Now, where are those hairy snakes?"

"You seek a monster named Medusa," Enyo answered. "She is a Gorgon, a creature with snakes for hair. She lives on an island west of here. If you leave now, you should reach it by sunset."

Athena gasped. "Snakes for hair! Just like the image on the aegis!"

"*Hairy snakes* . . . I get it now!" Hephaestus exclaimed.

"Give me the eye, boy," Enyo demanded. When Perseus handed it over, she eyed Athena's shield. "That shiny thing is an aegis?"

"Yes," Athena replied. "Sometimes an image of a woman with snakes for hair appears on it. And when that happens, the aegis can turn things to stone."

"That makes sense," said Enyo, "because, you see, if you—"

"Hey! Where's my cane!" Hephaestus wailed.

Zeus looked down. The silver cane, the aegis, the helmet, and Bolt too . . . they were all gone!

"Perseus!" Zeus yelled, whirling around. But the boy was nowhere in sight.

Enyo cackled. "Looks like your little friend is quite the clever thief."

"We can't let him get away!" Zeus yelled. Perseus had Bolt. *Bolt!* "Let's go!" he yelled.

"Wait! Enyo was telling us about Medusa—" Athena started to protest. But Zeus grabbed her arm and the four Olympians ran out of the cave.

CHAPTER SIX

Medusa

By the time Zeus, Hephaestus, Athena, and Hades reached the shore, Perseus was already out to sea, steering the ship farther and farther away from the island. Zeus splashed into the water after him, then stopped, realizing he'd never catch up. He watched helplessly as Perseus smiled wickedly and waved as he disappeared from view.

With doubled up fists Zeus struck the water

in frustration and then trudged back to shore. "I *knew* we should never have trusted that guy," he muttered to the others.

"It's okay, Zeus," Athena said. "At least we know where to find the hairy snakes now."

"Think Perseus is after the hairy snakes too?" Hephaestus asked. "Or did he just trick us so he could steal our boat and stuff?"

"Maybe he's on some kind of quest of his own," Athena suggested.

"I don't think he's an Olympian, though," Hades said.

"Of course not! He's a crummy thief!" Zeus shouted, angrily kicking the sand.

"We can still get to Medusa's island without the boat," Athena said. "We just need to make a raft."

"Oh sure, we'll just make a raft," Zeus said crossly. "No problem. Has anyone here ever made a raft?"

"You know, if I were Poseidon, I'd be telling you to chill out right now, Bro," Hades said. "Perseus may have stolen our weapons, but we can't let him steal our, you know, togetherness, right?"

Hephaestus shook his head. "Dude, for the ruler of a dark place like the Underworld, you sure know how to look on the bright side."

Hades shrugged. "If we use our heads, I think we still have a chance to catch up to Perseus. We can't let him get away with our stuff!"

"Gather some branches," Athena instructed the boys. "And some vines. I have an idea."

Knowing how clever she was, they didn't waste time questioning her. They all got to work gathering branches and long, green vines from farther inland. After they had gathered a big pile of them onshore, Athena took out her Thread of Cleverness, which she had managed to hide from the Gray Triplets. Then she unwound enough of the thread to shape the cursive word "raft" in big, loopy connected letters on the sand.

"Oh, I get it," Hades approved, realizing what she had planned.

Slowly the branches started to magically arrange themselves on the sand side by side in rows to form a flat platform about six feet square. Then the vines snaked and curled between the branches, tying the raft together.

Zeus was impressed. "Wow, that actually looks seaworthy," he said, giving Athena's raft a thumbs-up.

Athena grinned at him. "Good. Now let's get out of here. We've got a thief to catch."

Zeus touched Chip. "Point us due west!" At his command a green directional arrow appeared on the stone.

After launching their raft the Olympians

hopped aboard to sit or kneel and used their hands to paddle across the water. Luckily the sea was calm. By now, Perseus and their boat had already disappeared. Zeus knew there was no way the raft could overtake the boat, but his team kept going.

A few hours later, just as the sun began to set, an island came into view. "That's got to be it!" said Zeus. "See?" He showed them how Chip's arrow had just turned bright red and was spinning around in circles.

An eerie quiet greeted their ears once they reached the shore.

"Look! There's our boat!" Hades exclaimed. Perseus had tied the stolen boat to a nearby tree. Oddly it wasn't the only boat there. There were dozens, all empty.

"That's weird," Athena mused. "Judging from all these boats, there should be lots of people on this island. But it's so . . . quiet."

"Maybe everyone's asleep?" Hephaestus muttered.

"Hey! Are those trees?" Zeus asked. He pointed at hundreds of upright forms that stood planted in the sand some distance away.

"I don't think so," Hades replied, squinting at them. "Trees don't have faces."

Cautiously they walked up to the nearest one and saw that it was actually a statue. It was a gray stone statue of a man, his mouth open in terror.

Athena shuddered. "These are the weirdest statues I've ever seen. Why are they all silently screaming?"

"Is this some kind of outdoor art museum?" Hades asked.

Zeus got a prickly feeling on his skin. "If it is, I'm sure it doesn't get many visitors. It's super-creepy."

"I hate to interrupt your discussion of fine art, but I'd like to remind everyone that I don't have my cane. And you guys don't have your magical weapons," said Hephaestus. "What are we supposed to do when we find Medusa and her snakes? How are we supposed to defend ourselves if she attacks us?"

"We'll find Perseus first and get our weapons back," Zeus assured him. He ran over to the boat the boy had stolen.

"Look, there are his footprints!" Athena called out, pointing down at the sand. "Let's follow them."

The sun was sinking as the four Olympians walked deeper inland, following what they hoped was Perseus's trail. They traveled a well-worn path that sent them past a forest of more and more sinister statues.

After a while Athena hissed to the others,

"Has anybody noticed anything weird?"

"You mean besides all these creepy statues?" asked Hephaestus.

She nodded. "The ground seems to be shifting." The other Olympians looked down at the dirt.

"Uh-oh, don't look now, guys, but I don't think this is normal ground," said Hades. Suddenly a slimy creature seemed to material-ize from the sand itself, right next to Zeus. It raised its head and hissed, sticking out a forked pink tongue.

Zeus jumped back in horror. "Snake! Snake!" he cried. "This place is crawling with snakes!" The ground was covered with *hundreds* of the wriggling, writhing creatures. They were curl-ing up around the statues and the trees, too.

"Shh! Don't rile them up," Athena warned. "Just walk calmly down the path till we get to where we're going. Wherever that is."

Zeus forced himself to move down the path. It wasn't easy. But he was a leader and couldn't let his team down. They had no choice but to cautiously pick their way through and around the snakes.

"Ugh," he said. "I hope none of these reptiles mistake us for statues too and decide to coil around *us*!"

"Yeah," Hades said cheerfully. "If I ever need extra snakes for the Underworld, I know where to come."

"*Shhh!*" Athena said, pointing. "Look."

Up ahead of them the path opened into a clearing lit by flaming torches. The torches surrounded a small stone stage covered with statues. And every one of those statues had a frozen, terrified expression on its face.

Zeus did a double take when he saw that Perseus was tied with rope to one of the statues in the center of the stage! The boy's eyes were squeezed closed, and the Olympians' four magical objects were scattered at his feet.

A giant woman stood by him. She towered over the statues, wearing a green silk robe with a pattern of snakes stitched in black. Her back was to the Olympians as she faced Perseus. Though they couldn't see her face, her hair was a tangle of nasty black and green hissing serpents. Medusa, of course!

"That's one big lady," whispered Hades.

"Shh!" the other three Olympians hissed at him.

"Open your eyes, boy!" Medusa shrieked at Perseus. "We can do this the hard way or the easy way!"

"Never!" Perseus yelled.

Medusa grabbed a torch. "Maybe a little heat will convince you," she said wickedly.

"Perseus!" Athena wailed.

"Athena? Don't look into her eyes!" Perseus called out. "You'll be turned to stone like these other poor fools!"

Other poor fools? Fear gripped Zeus as he realized what Perseus meant. "Oh no! All these statues. They are real people Medusa turned into stone!"

Athena gasped. *"Which means she has the power to do in real life exactly what her image on the aegis can do!"*

At this, Hephaestus let out a terrified shriek. Medusa's head spun until the Olympians were fully within her sight. She snarled at them, and her eyes glowed an eerie red. Her red eyes locked with Zeus's gaze.

Instantly Zeus went stiff. He couldn't look away. He felt like he was . . . frozen!

CHAPTER SEVEN

The Monster's Weakness

"Y ou'll all make fine statues!" Medusa
crowed at the Olympians.

Are my three companions frozen too?
wondered Zeus. He couldn't move his head to
check. *It's happening!* he thought. *She's turning
us to stone! We'll never defeat King Cronus now.
And I'll never be the ruler of the Olympians!*

Then he noticed Medusa's puzzled frown,
and it suddenly hit him that he didn't *feel* like

stone. He broke away from Medusa's gaze and looked down at his hands.

They were flesh-and-blood hands. Not stone. Zeus slowly broke into a grin. He had only been scared stiff, not turned to stone after all.

"I guess your power doesn't work on gods," he told Medusa.

Hearing this, Athena, Hades, and Hephaestus opened their eyes. They all looked at Medusa.

"Hooray! We're not stone," cheered Hephaestus.

"Nooo faaaaiiiiir!" Medusa wailed. The snakes growing from her head all began to hiss.

Zeus and the other Olympians huddled together. "Give up! Your powers can't stop us, Medusa!" he called. "Free Perseus, and we'll go away and leave you alone."

"My gaze is only one of my powers," Medusa said darkly.

The slithery snakes on her head all turned

to look at the Olympians. Then they spoke as if they all shared one voice, just like the Gray Triplets shared an eye and a tooth! "Ussse thossse sssilly legsss of yours and come clossser," they chorused, "if you want to sssave your friend."

"Don't do it! Those snakes will eat us for dinner!" Hades warned in a loud whisper.

"Ssscaredy-godsssss! Ssscaredy-godsssss!" the snakes mocked.

Zeus thought quickly. A small part of him wanted to leave the thieving Perseus behind and run. But nobody deserved the fate that had befallen Medusa's other victims. And besides, the Olympians still needed to get back their magical objects.

Then it hit him. *Duh.* Bolt would come right to him if he called. "Bolt, come here!" Zeus yelled.

Right away the zigzag daggerlike object started

to glow. Then it jumped off the stage. But as it zipped through the air toward Zeus, one of the snakes on top of Medusa's head stretched out and wrapped itself tightly around Bolt. Caught!

"Nice try, lossser!" the snakes hissed at Zeus.

"Come and get your little toy weapon, if you want it," Medusa taunted them. Then she turned to Perseus, who kept his eyes shut tight.

"Your friends cannot help you, and they cannot defeat me," she said. "I can wait as long as you can, little mortal. Eventually you will be toast. Stone-cold toast!"

"Medusa, don't you dare put that helmet on Perseus before you turn him to stone," Athena said, nodding toward Hades's Helm of Darkness. "Even though he'd make a fine statue with it on."

Zeus knew what Athena was getting at. If Perseus wore the helmet, he would instantly become invisible—and then he could escape.

Provided he could get free of the rope binding him, too. However, surely this green Gorgon lady wasn't so dumb as to fall for Athena's trick.

Medusa's eyes narrowed. "And why should you care if I make him a fine statue, little goddess. Are you trying to trick me?"

Athena went on wrapping the thread around her finger. "How could I trick someone as smart as you?" she asked. "It's just . . . I'm surprised you are more interested in Perseus than the magical objects at your feet."

"And why should I be interested in those?" Medusa asked.

"Yessss, why?" echoed her head snakes.

"Because they are works of art," Athena said. "And I thought someone who makes magnificent sculptures like you do would appreciate them."

Medusa kicked the aegis, which was lying

facedown on the ground. "What do I care for your gold? Stone is far more beautiful!"

"Your stone sculptures *are* beautiful, in a grotesque kind of way," agreed Athena. "But the aegis is engraved with your image, you know."

Huh? The image wasn't exactly "engraved," thought Zeus. It only *sometimes* appeared, as Athena knew, of course. She seemed to have given up on the helmet idea. What was she up to now?

Medusa looked surprised . . . and flattered. "*My* image? Really?"

Although he wasn't quite sure where Athena was going with this, Zeus followed her lead. "Sure! People tell stories about you in every land. From the highest snowy mountaintops to the, um, bubbling hot springs."

"They do?" Medusa smiled and let out a pleased but horrible giggle. Her snakes wiggled and hissed happily, too.

"Yes," Athena said. "A great artist carved your image on that aegis. It doesn't do justice to your real beauty, but it's a very good likeness. Take a look."

Medusa seemed to forget her concern about being tricked. Eagerly she picked up the aegis. Its front side was turned away from her, but toward Zeus. He could see that her image had not appeared. But perhaps that didn't matter?

Medusa turned the gold aegis around. She looked directly into its shiny metal, and just like a mirror it reflected her face back to her. Only then did she realize the mistake she'd made. "Noooooo!" she screamed.

CHAPTER EIGHT

The Face in the Aegis

The Olympians watched as Medusa slowly transformed before their eyes. Gray stone formed at the ground, starting at the bottom of her cloak. It crept up her robe to her shoulders, then her neck.

"She's turning into a statue!" Hades yelled.

Zeus grinned at Athena. "You knew this would happen, didn't you?"

She nodded. "Medusa is a monster, not a

goddess. So, I hoped if she saw her image reflected in the aegis, it might turn her to stone!"

"Well, it's working!" cheered Hephaestus.

The Olympians watched as the gray took over her face and continued higher till it had stilled every wriggling snake on top of her head. She had completely turned to stone!

Now that she could no longer hurt them, the Olympians ran to help Perseus. Zeus pulled Bolt out of the tangle of stone snakes on Medusa's head and then sliced through Perseus's ropes. He was free!

Before they could stop him, the mortal grabbed Hades's helmet and put it on. Instantly he went invisible.

"Hey!" Hades protested. "Give that back!"

Zeus looked around for Perseus, but couldn't see him. "Where are you? And why do you keep stealing our magical objects?"

"I'll explain later," the invisible Perseus began. "But first . . ."

Hephaestus cried out. He had picked up his silver cane and was swinging it about wildly.

"Watch it!" Zeus yelled, ducking to avoid being hit.

"It's not me—my cane's swinging itself. Whoa, look out!" Hephaestus yelled as he tried to control the cane.

Suddenly it transformed into a silver sword! Hephaestus gave a yelp of surprise. "What's happening?" he cried. The sword pulled his arm back—and then swung forward.

Whack! The cane-sword sliced through the neck of the Medusa statue . . . and knocked her stone head off!

THUMP! It fell to the ground and rolled across the stage. For a second her eyes seemed to be looking right at Zeus. *Ick.* He shivered.

"How did I do that?" Hephaestus wondered in shock. As he gazed down at the sword in his hand it transformed back into a cane.

Perseus materialized beside him. "Hey, don't try to take credit, Hephaestus. While I was invisible *I* made your cane knock her block off. Who knew it would turn into a sword, though. That came in handy!"

Perseus tossed the helmet he'd removed from his head to Hades, who caught it. "Thanks for the loan!"

"You're not welcome," Hades replied, scowling.

Ignoring everyone, Perseus bent down and tried to pick up Medusa's stone head. When it proved too heavy, he broke off one of her stone hair snakes instead and pocketed it.

The real snakes on the ground had quieted for a while, but now they began to move and writhe again.

"Now you've done it! You woke them up!"

Hephaestus accused. Perseus only shrugged.

More and more snakes began to crawl all over Medusa's stone head where it lay on the ground, slithering in and out of her stiff snaky hair. Zeus shuddered.

"Something tells me we should get out of here—now," said Athena. She grabbed the aegis.

"Right. Let's go," urged Zeus. As he and his companions ran for their boat, hundreds more snakes streamed past them toward the stage. It seemed that all the island's snakes were going there to mourn Medusa.

"So, what's the deal with you stealing our stuff?" he asked Perseus again as they ran.

"I'm not normally a thief," Perseus protested.

Hades glared at him. "Really? You do a good impression of one."

"Well, I had a good reason for taking your stuff," argued Perseus. "Medusa has been terrorizing my land. She would come and turn people to stone and then disappear, and nobody knew where she lived."

"That explains why you needed us to take you to the Gray Triplets to get her address," Athena put in. "But why did you steal our objects?"

"The king of my land is cruel," Perseus said, and his voice grew sad. "He wants to marry my mom against her will!"

Zeus felt a pang. His father, King Cronus, was cruel too. But his mom, Rhea, was nice. It made him sad to think that Perseus's nice mom might have to marry a mean guy too.

Finally the Olympians and Perseus reached the shore. There were so many boats that they spread out to find the one with their belongings still on it. Zeus, Athena, and Perseus searched along the shore together. Hades and Hephaestus went the other direction.

"So, King Polydektes said that if I defeated Medusa, he wouldn't make my mom marry him," Perseus said. His eyes darkened. "He didn't think I could do it. But when I met you Olympians, I knew you had the right tools. Like the Helm of Darkness and Bolt. I put on the helmet and sneaked up on that Gorgon before you got here. I was going to clobber her with Bolt. But I tripped on a snake and fell. The helmet slid off, and I was caught."

"So your mom won't have to marry that cruel dorky king now, once you're back home?" Zeus asked.

Nodding, Perseus pulled something out of the pocket of his tunic and held it up. It was the stone snake that he'd broken off Medusa's hair. "This is my proof. The king won't go back on his word. At least I hope not."

"I get it," said Athena. "You had to help your

mom." She looked over at Zeus. "We understand. Right, Zeus?"

Yes, thought Zeus. He *did* understand. And
that meant that he couldn't stay mad at Perseus—
well, not *too* mad. Looking at the boy, he nodded. "Just don't steal from us again, okay?" he
said gruffly.

"I won't," Perseus said. Smiling now, he bent
to take off his winged sandals. "To prove it, I
want to give you these sandals. You can return
them to the guy I, uh, borrowed them from."

Athena watched curiously as Perseus handed
the sandals to Zeus.

Suddenly they heard a shout. Hades and
Hephaestus had found their boat. Zeus, Athena,
and Perseus turned and ran in their direction and
hopped aboard. Hades untied their boat and they
shoved off.

Zeus had never been happier to leave an island

in his entire life. Snakes were for the birds!

"Hey, where's Perseus?" Hephaestus asked, looking around.

"Over there!" Athena said, pointing across the sea. The mortal boy was busily rowing it away from the shore in a different direction. "He stayed behind without us noticing. And then jumped into one of the other deserted boats."

"Good riddance," muttered Hades.

Looking down at the winged sandals, Zeus suddenly remembered something. "Wait, I thought you said you *traded* for the sandals!" he called to Perseus. "Now you say you borrowed them?"

"Oh, well, maybe I sort of stole them actually," Perseus called back. "For a good cause. To defeat Medusa. Only I never could get the sandals to fly. Anyway, just return them to the thirteenth Olympian for me, okay?"

Zeus, Athena, Hades, and Hephaestus looked

at one another in surprise. As far as they knew, there were only twelve Olympians.

"What thirteenth Olympian?" Athena yelled.

Perseus was busy with his boat and didn't reply right away. Finally he called back over his shoulder, "Sorry, didn't get his name! Thanks for helping me. I hope you can find your friends again!"

"But where can we find this new Olympian?" Zeus called after him. Unfortunately Perseus was too far away to hear by now.

Zeus turned back to the others. "So I guess we're not done looking for Olympians!"

"Guess not," said Athena. She loosened the ties on her cloak so she could slip the aegis back over her neck. Suddenly she gasped. "Medusa's face! It's back on the aegis!"

CHAPTER NINE

The Mysterious Horse

I t's different from how it looked before, though," Athena said, gazing into the shield she wore. "It's like she's . . . *alive* somehow. The snakes on her head are wriggling. See?"

She turned the shield around to show the boys. Zeus saw Medusa's head all right—but her snakes looked perfectly still to him.

"It's wicked-looking, but nothing's moving," said Hades.

That confirmed what Zeus had seen—or rather, *not* seen. Was it possible Athena had only imagined the shield snakes wriggling?

"I don't see why everybody is so gaga over that dumb shield. Let's talk about how my cane turned into a *sword*," Hephaestus interjected. He thumped his cane against the boat deck for emphasis. "You all saw it slice through stone! Wasn't it cool?"

Athena nodded, going over to it and running her fingers over the carvings on the cane. "Yes, that whole thing was weird. It was like your cane had a mind of its own."

After Hephaestus took his cane back to lean on again, she turned the aegis to face her. "I wonder if, now that she's dead, her image on my shield will still turn things to stone?"

As she was speaking Zeus noticed what appeared to be a small rock sitting on the edge of the boat. He picked it up and looked at it closely. It wasn't a rock, after all. It was a beetle—made of stone!

"Here's your answer," Zeus said, handing the bug to her. "It must have looked into the shield when you showed it to us."

Athena frowned. "Sorry, beetle," she said sadly. "I wish I knew how to change you back."

She gazed around at the island. "If we see Pythia again, we should ask her if there's some way to turn return Medusa's victims back to flesh and blood," she said. "I feel sorry for all those people."

Zeus went over and grabbed an oar to begin paddling. "We'll ask her. I guess we should just feel lucky that Medusa's powers didn't work on *us*, or we could be statues now too." He shuddered. "Come on. There's not much wind for the sails, so let's paddle and get out of this creepy place."

"I'm a fan of creepy, but this place is too creepy even for me," Hades declared. He grabbed an oar too.

As they rowed away from the island, Athena put the aegis back on and covered it with her cloak. "I'd better be extra careful with this thing from now on," she said. "Especially when we're around mortals."

"You and me both," Hephaestus said, staring at the cane in his lap. "What if my cane starts cutting off heads left and right?" He sounded more admiring than appalled as he said this idea, however.

"Pythia will probably know how to handle that," Hades told him. "She usually has answers."

"Hope she pops up soon," Hephaestus said, still gazing at his cane.

Suddenly a rumbling sound came from the

island they'd just left. The Olympians looked back toward it. Medusa's stone stage had broken free of the ground and was rising up into the air. Even now it was visible above all the tall stone statues.

"What's happening?" Athena wondered.

The stage started to shake. Then . . . *boom!* It, and everything on it, which must have included Medusa's stone body, exploded, splintering into a thousand small rocks! The Olympians gasped.

Once the dust cleared, they could see some kind of figure emerge from the rubble to hover in the air. It was a winged creature of some sort.

"What is THAT?" Hades asked nervously.

As the Olympians stared at it, the figure flew high into the sky. "It's a white, winged horse!" Athena exclaimed.

"And it's diving straight at us!" yelled Hades. "Hit the deck!"

Instinctively Zeus pulled Bolt from his belt. Was this winged horse some kind of Creature of Chaos? Eager for action, the bolt sizzled and sparked as Zeus held it high.

Instead of being scared off, the horse gave a gentle whinny and swooped down, so low that they could almost touch it! It was beautiful, its coat glossy. It locked eyes with Zeus, and for a second he got a strange feeling . . . like he knew this horse somehow. Like they had met before. But of course they hadn't.

The horse whinnied again. Then it ducked its head and stretched its long neck toward him, so that they were almost nose to nose. It seemed friendly. However, just as Zeus reached up to pat it, the horse chomped down on Bolt and pulled it right from his hand!

"Noooo! Bolt!" Zeus yelled as the white horse flew away.

CHAPTER TEN

Where Is Pythia?

Bolt, return!" Zeus yelled. But Bolt did not. Rising high into the sky, the horse flew quickly over the water, and then disappeared into the distance.

"Booolt!" Zeus drew out the word in a mournful voice. Then he dropped his head in defeat. What would he do without his trusty magical object?

Athena put a hand on his shoulder. "Hey. It's

okay," she said gently. "You've lost Bolt before, right? But you found him again. I'm sure Bolt's not lost forever."

Hephaestus grabbed an oar and began paddling. "We need to get as far away from this island as possible. It's even weirder than the one I used to live on!"

"Yeah, let's vamoose," said Hades. He and Athena fiddled with the sail until it caught some wind. Soon they were whipping across the sea.

Zeus grabbed Chip. "Follow that horse!" he commanded. "We need to find that winged horse and get Bolt."

"Is-thip ay-wip!" the magic stone replied, and a green, glowing arrow appeared on its surface. *This way.*

"But, Zeus," Athena said. "We're supposed to meet the others back in the village. They might be waiting for us."

Zeus paused. Athena was right. But that horse was getting farther and farther away with every second.

"I'll do whatever you want," Hades piped up. "I mean, I'm sure the other Olympians will understand if we're delayed."

Zeus wasn't so sure. He could practically hear Hera's voice in his head. *Where were you, Bolt-breath? We waited here for you for days. We're supposed to be going on quests, not chasing after flying horses!*

Zeus sighed. "All right," he said. "We'll go back to the village." He bent over Chip again. "Which way?" he asked.

Chip's arrow glowed.

"Hey, Chip's still pointing in the same direction," Hades said. "Toward where the horse went! That's a galloping great coincidence, if you ask me."

Zeus felt a little better. "Onward!" he cried out.

Luckily there was a good wind at their backs. They glided swiftly through the water, with Chip's arrow guiding the way. Later, it grew darker, but there was no way to light their way without Bolt.

As a bright moon rose overhead, they spotted the island meeting place. "Almost there!" Zeus called out.

Zeus and Hephaestus rowed the rest of the way to shore. When the boat hit the sand, they all straggled out, exhausted and hungry.

"It's too late to find the village now," Hades said. "We should camp here."

"But we can't make a fire," Zeus said sadly, remembering Bolt again.

"It's a warm night," Athena reassured him. "And we've got the bread and cheese we bought before in the village to eat. Come on. Let's find a spot."

They marched away from the shore for a bit, so they wouldn't be caught when the tide came in. When they found some clear, level ground, they unpacked their food, blankets, and water. As they emptied the bags Zeus realized he was still carrying the winged sandals Perseus had given him.

"I wonder who these belong to," he mused.

"Maybe one of us could wear them?" Hades suggested. "I mean, my helmet works on whoever wears it, so why not the sandals? I wouldn't mind flying around instead of hiking everywhere."

Zeus grinned and handed them to Hades. "Go for it!"

Hades kicked off his own sandals and tried to wiggle one of the winged sandals onto his foot. He got it halfway on and held up his foot. His entire heel was hanging off the back of the sandal.

"Too small," he said with disappointment.

"Let me try," Hephaestus said, taking the sandals from him. But he didn't have any better luck. "*Way* too small."

"Guess your new nickname should be Hephaestus Littlefoot," Hades said, laughing. Then he yelled, "Ow!" Hephaestus's cane had whacked him on the back of the head!

"Sorry," Hephaestus replied earnestly. "I can't seem to control this cane anymore." But Zeus wasn't totally sure if that was true this time.

"My turn!" said Athena. She was able to get both sandals onto her feet. But when she took a step, her feet slipped right out! She laughed. "They're a little too big for me."

She handed the sandals to Zeus. "How about you?" she asked.

"I'll try, but something tells me . . ." he said, trying to slip one onto his foot. He shook his head. "Too small!"

"So, I guess we're looking for a boy with small feet or a girl with large feet," Athena said. "Wait, Perseus said the Olympian was a 'him,' didn't he?"

"Yeah! And maybe he made a mistake about there being a thirteenth Olympian. I mean, maybe these sandals will fit Poseidon, Ares, or Apollo," said Hades. Reminded of their missing friends, everyone suddenly got quiet.

"Pythia would tell us, if she were here," Zeus said.

"She'll probably appear tomorrow," Athena said encouragingly. "Come on. We should get some rest."

The four Olympians quickly fell asleep and woke up with the morning sun.

"Pythia?" Zeus called out once they'd eaten and were ready to move out, but she was nowhere to be seen. He frowned at the others. "The last time Pythia went missing, it was because she was captured by a huge python. I hope nothing bad has happened to her again."

"Maybe she's waiting to show herself until we're all together again," Athena suggested. "Let's get to the village. I bet everyone beat us there already."

"That was some crazy flying horse last night," Hades said as they marched off together. "I hate to be a *naaay*sayer, but I don't think that thing was very *stable*."

Hephaestus and Athena groaned, but Zeus laughed. "Very *punny*," he said. "I haven't heard you make a bad joke in a while.'"

Hades smiled. "I'm feeling pretty good today. We destroyed the monstrous Medusa, and we'll be seeing everybody else soon."

"Do you always express your happiness through really bad jokes?" Hephaestus asked.

Hades grinned. "Not always. Sometimes when

I'm happy I ask myself serious questions. Like, do you know why I don't trust stairs?"

Hephaestus shrugged. "Why?"

"Because they're always *up* to something," Hades said, cracking himself up. "Get it?"

Hephaestus groaned even more loudly this time.

"Well, besides not trusting stairs, I just plain don't like them," Athena remarked. "They always bring me *down*."

Zeus and Hades laughed so hard they almost *fell* down.

"I can't take much more of this," Hephaestus said, rolling his eyes. "How far is it to the village?"

"Not far," Zeus said, and he found himself smiling again.

Hades was his brother, but Athena and even Hephaestus also felt like family now. So did all the other Olympians. Even if the winged white horse hadn't been flying in the same direction, he would have chosen to return to the village, he knew. It was the right thing to do. It was important to keep all of them together.

If I ever lost my siblings and friends, I think I'd lose myself, he thought. Still, he couldn't help feeling a pang when his hand touched his belt, where Bolt used to hang.

The thought that all twelve Olympians would soon be together again comforted him. *Then Pythia will appear and tell us what to do next,* he told himself. *And I will get Bolt back, if it's the last thing I do!*